The Very Droopy Honey Bear

Written and illustrated by Mama Bear Gina

For my real life honey bears: Erica and Signe

The Very Droopy Honey Bear

iUniverse books may be ordered through booksellers or by contacting:

iUniverse
1663 Liberty Drive
Bloomington, IN 47403
www.iuniverse.com
1-800-Authors (1-800-288-4677)

Because of the dynamic nature of the Internet, any web addresses or links contained in this book may have changed since publication and may no longer be valid. The views expressed in this work are solely those of the author and do not necessarily reflect the views of the publisher, and the publisher hereby disclaims any responsibility for them.

ISBN: 978-1-5320-6731-0 (sc)
ISBN: 978-1-5320-6732-7 (e)

Library of Congress Control Number: 2019900954

Print information available on the last page.

iUniverse rev. date: 02/26/2019

The Very Droopy Honey Bear

Very Droopy Honey Bear wasn't always

so,

well,

Droopy.

1

He warmed up in the microwave often

and each time came back sadder

and emptier

and, well,

Droopier. He never spoke, or sang, or looked up. He only sighed.

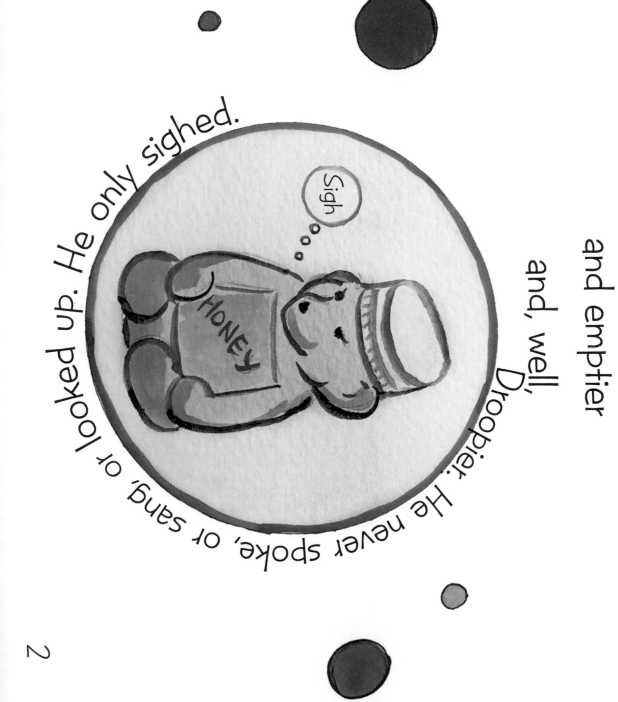

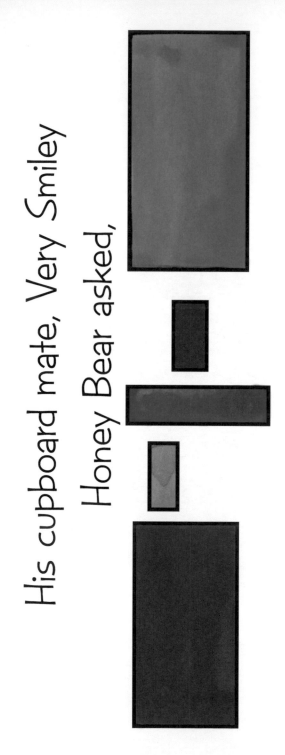

His cupboard mate, Very Smiley
Honey Bear asked,

3

"Very Droopy Honey Bear,

why are you so sad?"

"I must have been bad."

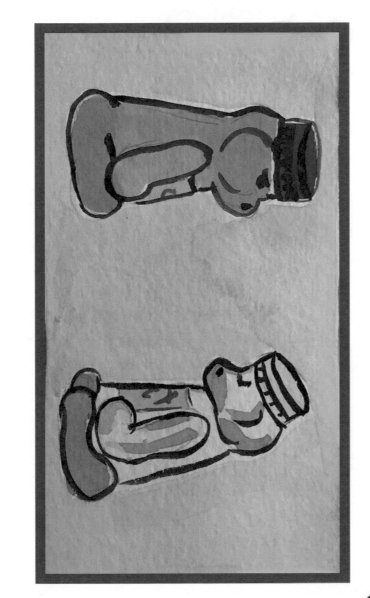

Very Smiley Honey Bear looked

down at Droopy Bear's feet.

"Oh," she said. She saw only the flat, hard table.

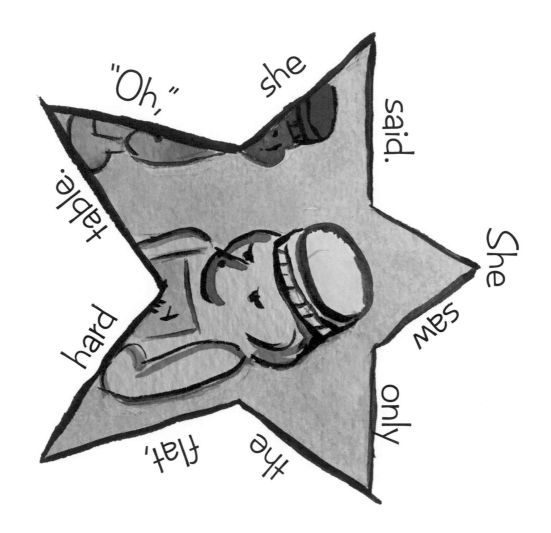

Very Smiley Honey Bear looked all around her at the happy kitchen,

at the yummy ginger honey cookies,

and the honey wheat bread.

8

She asked,
"Very Droopy Honey Bear,

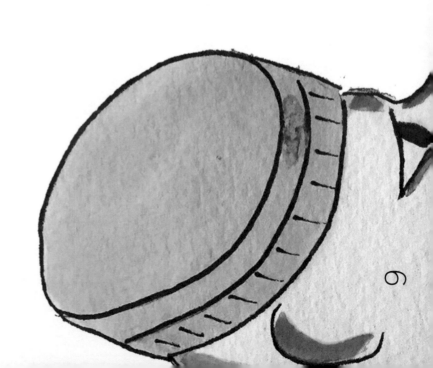

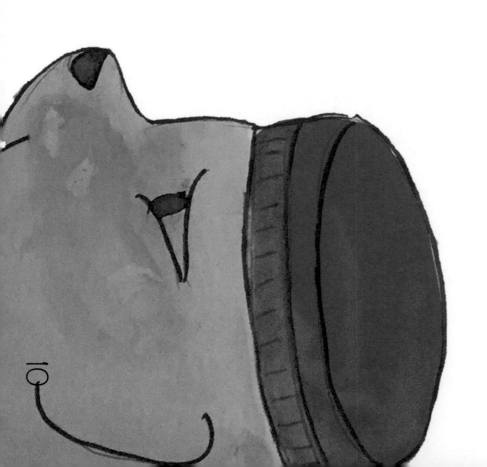

What do you SEE?"

10

"I only see

what is below me."

Very Smiley Honey Bear
HEARD the humming
of the little girl
and her friend.

And
she
smiled
again.

"Very Droopy Honey Bear, what do you HEAR?"

"I hear the microwave."

Very Smiley Honey Bear (who had never been to the microwave) began to feel herself getting Droopy.

But then she felt the warmth of the kitchen and the warmth of the gentle fingers holding her.

She asked, "Very Droopy
Honey Bear,

What do you FEEL?"

"I feel empty," he said.

"Oh! Oh dear," she said

But, just
then,

Very Smiley
Honey
Bear felt
herself
being
lifted
and
tipped.

"Upsy Daisy!" she heard the little girl say.

"Careful!" she heard the boy say.

And she saw Droopy Bear
UPSIDE DOWN!

The next thing she knew,
she and Very Droopy Honey
Bear were EVEN STEVEN!

She was
still Happy

He was not
so Droopy.

She TASTED a drop of honey
as it dripped past her mouth.

She SMELLED the honey
cream on the warm hands.

She HEARD Very Very Droopy Honey Bear say,

"I'm FEELING a little Happy!"

Very Smiley Honey Bear said,

"Very Droopy Honey Bear, I can share!"

He said, "Thank you. I know that you care."

And they were both tipped up

to sweeten two cups of tea

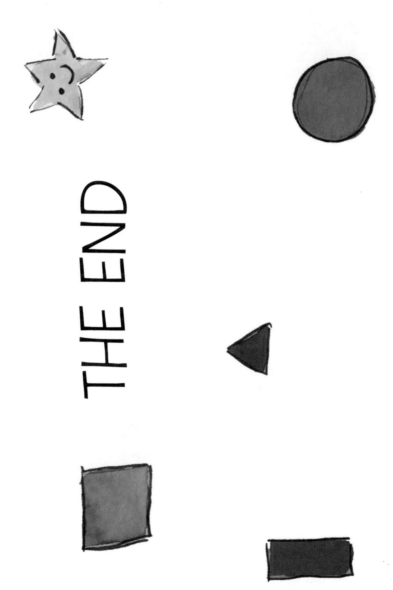

THE END

Printed in the United States
By Bookmasters